THIS BOOK

BELONGS

TO

1911 OHIO DOMINICAN COLLEGE

LIBRARY

**1216 SUNBURY RD.
COLUMBUS, OHIO**

Donated By:
  Martha Galloway
        Petrucci   '56

Gift of

ALEXANDER THE GANDER

Tasha Tudor

HENRY Z. WALCK, INCORPORATED

New York

ANOTHER WEE STORY
FOR
SYLVIE

ONE DAY SYLVIE ANN TOOK WIGGY AND HER TWO GEESE, ALEXANDER AND ARAMINTA, FOR A WALK TO THE POND.

ON THE WAY THEY PASSED Mrs. Fillow's house. Mrs. Fillow was setting out heliotrope pansies in her garden.

ALEXANDER WAS VERY
FOND OF HELIOTROPE PANSIES
TOO, AND STUCK HIS LONG
NECK THROUGH THE FENCE TO
SEE IF HE COULD REACH SOME.

SHOOH, SHOOH! YOU NAUGHTY GANDER, SAID SYLVIE, AND SHE HAD TO FLAP HER PINAFORE AT HIM BEFORE HE WOULD LEAVE THE FENCE AND COME WALKING.

WHEN SYLVIE AND WIGGY
AND ALEXANDER AND ARAMINTA
CAME TO THE POND, SYLVIE ANN
TOOK HER SHOES AND STOCKINGS
OFF AND WENT WADING.

IGGY WENT TO HUNT FROGS AMONG THE LILY PADS.

ND ALEXANDER AND ARAMINTA SWAM TO THE MIDDLE OF THE POND TO DABBLE FOR POND WEEDS.

BUT ALEXANDER JUST COULDN'T FORGET THOSE HELIOTROPE PANSIES!

He SWAM TO THE BUSHES AT THE EDGE OF THE POND AND LOOKED AROUND.

E SNEAKED AWAY AND STARTED UP THE ROAD MAKING FLAT, DAMP FOOTMARKS IN THE SOFT DUST.

WHEN ALEXANDER CAME IN SIGHT OF MRS. FILLOW'S HOUSE, HE TOOK A SHORT CUT BY WAY OF THE VEGETABLE GARDEN. "FOR", THOUGHT ALEXANDER, "I MIGHT JUST AS WELL TRY A FEW YOUNG CARROTS AND LETTUCES, AND FINISH OFF WITH HELIOTROPE PANSIES FOR DESSERT".

E WAS VERY CAREFUL TO MAKE SURE MRS. FILLOW DIDN'T SEE HIM.

Luckily THE GARDEN GATE WAS OPEN. HE WALKED IN AND BEGAN WITH A ROW OF LETTUCE SEEDLINGS.

THEN THREE HILLS OF YOUNG BEAN PLANTS, WITH A WEE BIT OF CABBAGE HERE AND THERE TO ADD FLAVOUR.

WHEN HE HAD ENOUGH HE WALKED UP THE LANE PAST THE CURRANT BUSHES AND ACROSS SOME NEWLY WASHED TABLECLOTHS TO MRS. FILLOW'S FLOWER GARDEN.

RS. FILLOW WAS NOWHERE
IN SIGHT. ALEXANDER QUACKED
WITH ANTICIPATION AS HE SAW
THE NEAT ROWS OF HELIOTROPE
PANSIES.

"JUST WAITING TO BE
GOBBLED UP", THOUGHT ALEXANDER.

BUT MRS. FILLOW THOUGHT
QUITE DIFFERENTLY, AS THAT
MOMENT SHE DISCOVERED HIM
FROM HER KITCHEN WINDOW!

HE SHRIEKED AT ALEXANDER AND FRIGHTENED HIM SO BADLY THAT HE THOUGHT OF FEATHER BEDS AND ROAST GOOSE BOTH AT ONCE.

OU CAN IMAGINE THAT ALEXANDER LEFT VERY ABRUPTLY, BY WAY OF A ROSE TRELLIS.

JUST THEN SYLVIE AND WIGGY AND ARAMINTA CAME BACK FROM THE POND LOOKING FOR HIM. THEY FOUND HIM HURRYING ACROSS THE PASTURE TOWARDS HOME.

YLVIE AND WIGGY RAN AFTER ALEXANDER AND CAUGHT HIM, AND BROUGHT HIM BACK TO APOLOGIZE TO MRS. FILLOW FOR DOING SUCH NAUGHTY THINGS.

LEXANDER HUNG HIS HEAD AND LOOKED DREADFULLY ASHAMED, SO Mrs. Fillow PARDONED HIM BECAUSE SHE WAS VERY NICE.

HEN Mrs. Fillow WENT
TO THE KITCHEN AND CAME
BACK WITH CAMBRIC TEA AND
COOKIES, FOR HERSELF AND
SYLVIE, AND SOME STALE
BISCUITS FOR WIGGY AND
ALEXANDER AND ARAMINTA.

THEY ALL SAT ABOUT
THE DOORSTEP AND ENJOYED
THEIR TEA VERY MUCH.

UT I AM AFRAID ALEXANDER NEVER FELT PROPERLY SORRY FOR WHAT HE DID, BECAUSE HE STILL HAS A DREADFUL FONDNESS FOR YOUNG VEGETABLES, AND ESPECIALLY FOR HELIOTROPE PANSIES, AND EATS THEM WHENEVER SOMEONE FORGETS TO CLOSE THE GARDEN GATE.

THE END